Ms Wiz Spells Trouble

Terence Blacker was born in 1948 and lives in London with his wife and two children. He worked in publishing for several years before becoming a full-time writer in 1983, since when he has written several books for adults and children. Apart from the *Ms Wiz* series, his children's books include *If I Could Work*, *Henry and the Frights*, *Here's Houdini* and a modern version of *The Surprising Adventures of Baron Munchausen*. *Ms Wiz Spells Trouble* was shortlisted for the Children's Book Award 1988 and selected for the *Children's Books of the Year 1989*: 'The sparkling, zany humour lights up this story from the very beginning . . . Terence Blacker's skilful writing has resulted in a brilliantly funny book.'

Ms Wiz Spells Trouble was shortlisted for the 1989 Children's Book Award (Sponsored by the Federation of Children's Book Groups). This is what the judges, aged between 7 and 13, had to say:

'I found *Ms Wiz Spells Trouble* hilarious, especially the bit about the owl.'

'I liked it because we are in class three and it's about class three. Mrs Cooper has brown eyes so has Ms Wiz so it's very much like our class and if Mrs Cooper was magic I would like her to turn class four into pigs.'

'The book is very funny, the words are easy to understand, the story is always exciting and the illustrations are great.'

'I gave it 10 out of 10 because I think it's brilliant.'

'One of the funniest books I have ever read.'

'Ms Wiz is the greatest, yeah.'

The other books in the Ms Wiz series are:
In Stitches with Ms Wiz
You're Nicked, Ms Wiz
In Control, Ms Wiz?
Ms Wiz Goes Live
Ms Wiz Banned!

Titles to follow

Time Flies for Ms Wiz
Power-crazy Ms Wiz

Terence Blacker

Ms Wiz Spells Trouble

Illustrated by Toni Goffe

YOUNG
PIPER

First published 1988 by Piccadilly Press Ltd

This Young Piper edition published 1989 by Pan Books,
Cavaye Place, London SW10 9PG

9 8 7

© Text Terence Blacker 1988
© Illustrations Toni Goffe 1988

ISBN 0 330 31096 8

Printed and bound in Great Britain by
Cox & Wyman Ltd, Reading

For Alice

Chapter One

A New Arrival

Most teachers are strange and the teachers at St Barnabas School were no exception.

Yet it's almost certain that none of them – not Mr Gilbert, the headmaster, who liked to pick his nose during Assembly, not Mrs Hicks who talked to her teddies in class, not Miss Gomaz who smoked cigarettes in the lavatory – *none* of them was quite as odd as the new form teacher for Class Three.

Some of the children in Class Three thought she was a witch. Others said she was a hippy. A few of them thought she was just a bit mad. But they all agreed that there had never been anyone quite like her at St Barnabas before.

This is her story. I wonder what *you* think she was . . .

As soon as their new teacher walked into the classroom on the first day of term, the children of Class Three sensed that there was something different about her. She was quite tall, with long black hair and bright green eyes. She wore tight jeans and a purple blouse. Her fingers were decorated with several large rings and black nail varnish. She looked as if she were on her way to a disco, not teaching at a school.

Most surprising of all, she wasn't frightened. Class Three was known in the school as the 'problem class'. It had a reputation for being difficult and noisy, for having what was called a 'disruptive element'. Miss Jones, their last teacher, had left the school in tears. But none of that seemed to worry this strange-looking new teacher.

'My name is Miss Wisdom,' she said in a quiet but firm voice. 'So what do you say to me every morning when I walk in?'

'Good morning, Miss Wisdom,' said Class Three unenthusiastically.

'Wrong,' said the teacher with a flash of her green eyes. 'You say, "Hi, Ms Wiz!"'

3

Jack, who was one of Class Three's Disruptive Element, giggled at the back of the class.

'Yo,' he said in a silly American accent. 'Why, hi Ms Wiz!'

Caroline, the class dreamer, was paying attention for a change.

'Why is it Ms . . . er, Ms?' she asked.

'Well,' said Ms Wiz, 'I'm not Mrs because I'm not married, thank goodness, and I'm not Miss because I think Miss sounds silly for a grown woman, don't you?'

'Not as silly as Ms,' muttered Katrina, who liked to find fault wherever possible.

'And why Wiz?' asked a rather large boy sitting in the front row. It was Podge, who was probably the most annoying and certainly the greediest boy in the class.

'Wiz?' said Ms Wiz with a mysterious smile. 'Just you wait and see.'

Ms Wiz reached inside a big leather bag that she had placed beside her desk. She pulled out a china cat.

'That,' she said, placing the cat carefully on her desk, 'is my friend Hecate the Cat. She's watching you all the time. She sees everything and hears everything. She's my spy.'

Ms Wiz turned to the blackboard.

'Weird,' muttered Jack.

An odd, hissing sound came from the china cat. Its eyes lit up like torches.

'Hecate sees you even when my back is turned,' said Ms Wiz, who now faced the class. 'Will the person who said "weird" spell it please?'

Everyone stared at Jack, who blushed.

'I.T.,' he stammered.

No one laughed.

'Er, W . . . I . . .'

'Wrong,' said Ms Wiz. 'W.E.I.R.D. If you don't know how to spell a word, Jack, don't use it.' She patted the china cat.

'Good girl, Hecate,' she said.

'How did she know my name?' whispered Jack.

The new teacher smiled. 'Children, remember one thing. Ms Wiz knows everything.'

'Now,' she said briskly. 'Pay attention, please. Talking of spelling, I'm going to give you a first lesson in casting spells.'

'Oh, great,' said Katrina grumpily. 'Now we've got a witch for a teacher.'

Hecate the Cat hissed angrily.

'No, Katrina, not a witch,' said Ms Wiz sharply. 'We don't call them witches these days. It gives people the wrong idea. We

call them Paranormal Operatives. Now –
any suggestions for our first spell?'

Podge put up his hand immediately.

'Could we turn our crayons into
lollipops, please Ms?' he asked.

'No,' said Ms Wiz. 'Spells are not for
personal greed.'

'How about turning Class Two into
frogs?' asked Katrina.

'Nor are they for revenge. There will be
no unpleasant spells around here while
I'm your teacher,' said Ms Wiz before
adding, almost as an afterthought, 'unless
they're deserved, of course.'

She looked out of the window. In the
playground Mr Brown, the school
caretaker, was sweeping up leaves.

'Please draw the playground,' said Ms
Wiz. 'Imagine it without any leaves. The
best picture will create the spell.'

Almost for the first time in living
memory, Class Three worked in complete
quiet. Katrina didn't complain that

someone had nicked her pencil. Caroline managed to concentrate on her work. Podge forgot to look in his trouser pocket for one last sweet. Not a single paper pellet was shot across the room by Jack.

At the end of the lesson, Ms Wiz looked at the drawings carefully.

'Well, they're all quite good,' she said eventually. 'But I think I like Caroline's the best.'

She took Caroline's drawing and carefully taped it to the window.

'Please close your eyes while I cast the spell,' she said.

There was a curious humming noise as Class Three sat, eyes closed, in silence.

'Open,' said Ms Wiz, after a few seconds. 'Regard Caroline's work.'

The children looked at Caroline's drawing. It looked exactly as it had before, except that it was steaming slightly.

'Hey – look at the playground!' shouted

Katrina.

Everyone looked out of the window. To their amazement, the leaves on the ground had disappeared. Mr Brown stood by his wheelbarrow, scratching his head.

'Weird,' said Jack. 'Very weird indeed.'

Chapter Two

'Ms Wiz is Magic'

'Yes, I'm afraid she is a bit odd,' sighed the headmaster, Mr Gilbert, as he took tea one morning with Miss Gomaz and Mrs Hicks in the Staff Common Room.

'Those jeans,' sniffed Miss Gomaz. 'And I never thought I'd live to see *black* nail-varnish at St Barnabas.'

'But you have to admit she seems to have Class Three under control,' said Mr Gilbert. 'That's a whole week she has been here and not one child has been sent to my study. Not one window has been broken.'

Mrs Hicks stirred her tea disapprovingly.

'It won't last,' she said. 'The Disruptive Element will get the better of her. And there are some very strange noises coming from that classroom.'

'I'd keep an eye on the situation if I were you, headmaster,' said Miss Gomaz.

Mr Gilbert sighed.

'Yes,' he said wearily. 'That's what I'll do. Keep an eye on the situation.'

The fact is that Class Three, including the Disruptive Element, were having the time of their lives.

Every lesson with Ms Wiz was different.

'Now, Class Three,' she would say, 'I'm going to teach you something rather unusual. But remember – what happens in this classroom is our secret. The magic only works if nobody except us knows about it.' Surprisingly, Class Three agreed.

So no one – not even parents or other children at the school – had any idea of the strange things that happened to Class Three.

They never heard how Caroline's picture of the playground saved Mr Brown a morning's work.

They never heard how Jack's desk moved to the front of the class all by itself when Hecate spotted him talking at the back.

They never heard how Katrina flew around the class three times on a vacuum cleaner after she had complained that Ms Wiz couldn't be a real witch – sorry, Paranormal Operative – because she didn't ride a broomstick.

They never heard about the nature lesson when the class met Herbert, a pet rat that Ms Wiz kept up her sleeve.

But they did hear about the day when Podge became the hero of the class.

Nobody could keep *that* a secret.

Once every term, Class Three played a football match against a team from a school nearby, called Brackenhurst. It was a very important game and everyone from St Barnabas gathered in the playground to watch. Last term, Class Three had lost 10-0.

'That was because Miss Jones picked all the wimps,' explained Jack.

'Because she was a wimp herself,' said Caroline.

The rest of the class agreed noisily.

'*I'll* be manager,' shouted Jack over the din.

Ms Wiz held up her hands like a wizard about to cast a spell.

'I'll be manager,' she said firmly.

'But you don't know anything about football,' said Jack.

'Ms Wiz knows everything,' said Caroline.

'Creep!' muttered Katrina.

Hecate the Cat hissed angrily.

'All right, Hecate,' said Katrina quickly. 'I take it back.'

'My team,' said Ms Wiz, 'is Jack, Simon, Katrina, Alex and – ' She looked around the classroom and saw Podge's arm waving wildly.

'*No*, Ms Wiz,' several of the class shouted at once. 'Not Podge! He's useless!'

' – and Podge.'

There was a groan from around the classroom.

'Here comes another hammering,' said Jack gloomily.

For a while during the game that afternoon, it looked as though Jack's prediction had been right. After three minutes, Brackenhurst had already scored twice. Podge had been a disaster, falling over his own feet every time the ball came near him.

'Serves that Ms Cleverclogs right,' said Mrs Hicks, who was watching the match with Miss Gomaz. 'Look at her, jumping up and down like that, making herself look foolish in front of the kiddies. Anybody would think she was a child herself.'

'It's embarrassing, that's what it is,' agreed Miss Gomaz.

'*Do* something,' said Caroline who was standing next to Ms Wiz.

'And what do you suggest, Caroline?' asked Ms Wiz whose normally pale face was now quite red.

'You know,' whispered Caroline. 'Something *special*.'

'Oh, all right,' sighed Ms Wiz. 'I suppose a *little* magic wouldn't hurt.'

At that moment, Podge blundered into one of Brackenhurst's players and knocked him over. Mr Gilbert, who was referee, blew hard on his whistle for a free kick against Class Three – but not a sound came out. In fact, the only sound to be heard was a faint humming noise from the direction of Ms Wiz.

'That's better,' said Caroline.

Brackenhurst's players were still waiting for the whistle to blow when Podge set off with the ball at his feet. He took two paces and booted it wildly. It was heading several feet wide of the Brackenhurst goal when, to everyone's astonishment, the ball changed direction and, as if it had a life of its own, flew into the back of the net.

For a moment, there was a stunned silence. Then Ms Wiz could be heard cheering on her team once more.

'What a shot!' she shouted. 'Nice one, Podge!'

'Appalling behaviour,' muttered Mrs Hicks.

From then on, the game altered completely. Not even in his wildest dreams, when he had scored the winning goal for Spurs in the FA Cup Final, had Podge played so well. Soon even Jack was shouting, 'Give it to Podge! Give the ball to Podge!' while the Brackenhurst players were screaming, 'Stop the fat one! Trip him, someone!'

But nobody could stop Podge. Playing as if he were under a spell, he scored three goals to give Class Three a great 3-2 victory.

After the game, the class gathered around Ms Wiz, shouting, cheering and singing songs.

'So much for her having her class under control,' said Mrs Hicks. 'They may win matches but Class Three are worse than ever with the new teacher.'

Miss Gomaz had hurried over to Mr Gilbert.

'Just look at that, headmaster,' she said, pointing to Class Three, who were now singing 'Ms Wiz is magic!' at the top of their voices. 'It's nothing short of anarchy.'

But Mr Gilbert wasn't listening. He was still studying his new whistle and wondering why it hadn't worked.

Chapter Three

An Extremely Mathematical Owl

'This is all very difficult,' said Mr Gilbert, puffing nervously on his pipe. He was sitting in his study with Ms Wiz, who at this moment was looking at him with an annoying little smile on her face. 'Very awkward. You see, Miss Wisdom – er, Ms Wiz – there have been, well, complaints.'

'Goodness,' said Ms Wiz brightly. 'What on earth about?'

Mr Gilbert fumbled around with his pipe. Why *was* he feeling so nervous? Of course, he was always uneasy with women, but there were lots of women

who were more frightening than Ms Wiz
– Mrs Gilbert, for a start. The thought of
his wife made the headmaster sit up in his
armchair and try again.

'Firstly, there have been complaints
about the way you look,' he said, glancing
at Ms Wiz. She was actually wearing
black lipstick today.

'You find something wrong with the
way I look?' asked Ms Wiz, who was
beginning to be confused by this
conversation.

'No, no,' said Mr Gilbert, tapping his
pipe on an ashtray. 'I like . . . I mean,
I don't . . .personally . . . Then,' he said,
quickly changing the subject, 'there's
what you teach. Your history lessons, for
example.'

'But Class Three loves history,' said Ms Wiz. 'We're doing the French Revolution at the moment.'

'So I gather,' said Mr Gilbert. 'The entire class was walking around the playground yesterday shouting, "Behead the aristocrats!" I'm told that Jack was carrying a potato on the end of a sharp stick.'

Ms Wiz laughed. 'They're very keen,' she said.

'Perhaps you could move on to some other part of history – *nice* history,' said the headmaster. '1066, the Armada, King Alfred and the cakes.'

'Oh no,' said Ms Wiz. 'We already have our next project.'

'May I know what it is?' asked Mr Gilbert uneasily.

'Certainly,' said Ms Wiz. 'The Great Fire of London.'

The headmaster gulped. Mrs Hicks and Miss Gomaz had been right. Ms Wiz spelt trouble.

'Perhaps,' he said, 'you could concentrate on some other subject for the time being.'

'Of course,' said Ms Wiz. 'We'll try a spot of maths for a while.'

Mr Gilbert smiled for the first time that morning.

'Perfect,' he said.

Maths, he thought to himself after Ms Wiz had left his study. That couldn't cause trouble. Could it?

'Now, Class Three,' said Ms Wiz that afternoon. 'I'm going to test you on your nine times table – multiplication and division.'

There was a groan around the classroom. Nobody liked the nine times table.

'And to help me,' continued Ms Wiz, 'I've brought my friend Archimedes.' She reached inside her desk and brought out a large white owl. 'Archie's what they call a bit of a number-cruncher. He loves his tables,' she said, putting the owl on top of the blackboard.

'Cats, rats and now owls,' muttered Katrina. 'This place gets more like a zoo every day.'

'Archie is a barn owl,' said Ms Wiz, ignoring Katrina. 'An extremely mathematical barn owl. Place the waste-

paper basket beneath him please,
Caroline.'

'Why, Ms Wiz?' asked Caroline.

'Wait and see,' said Ms Wiz.

Caroline put the waste-paper basket
beneath Archie who was now looking
around the classroom, blinking wisely.

'Now Podge,' said Ms Wiz. 'Tell Archie
what five nines are.'

'Forty-five,' said Podge.

'Toowoo,' went Archie.

'That means correct,' said Ms Wiz.
'Simon – nine nines.'

'Eighty-one,' said Simon.

'Toowoo.'

'Now Jack,' said Ms Wiz. 'Let's try division. A boy has 108 marbles. He divides them between his nine friends. What does that make?'

'It makes him a wally for giving away all his marbles,' said Jack.

Archie looked confused.

'Try again, Jack,' said Ms Wiz patiently.

'Erm . . . eleven.'

Class Three looked at Archie expectantly. Without a sound, the owl lifted its tail and did something very nasty into the waste-paper basket beneath him.

'Uuuuuuuurrrrggghhhh, gross,' said the children. 'He's done a – '

'The correct word is guano,' said Ms Wiz. 'Jack?'

'Ten,' said Jack.

Archie lifted his tail.

'Eight.'

Archie did it again.

'How does he keep doing that?' asked Podge.

Ms Wiz shrugged. 'He's well-trained,' she said.

'We'd better have another basket standing by,' said Katrina. 'Jack's never going to get it.'

'He'd better,' said Ms Wiz firmly. 'Every time Archie is obliged to do his . . . guano, it means fifty lines.'

Jack groaned. 'Um . . .'

Outside the door Mrs Hicks and Miss Gomaz were listening carefully.

They had left their classes with some reading work and were determined to catch the new teacher doing something wrong.

'Listen to that noise,' said Miss Gomaz. 'It's an absolute disgrace.'

'Let's take a look through the window from the playground,' said Mrs Hicks.

Moments later, the two teachers were watching in amazement as Jack struggled to give Archie the correct answer.

'There's a bird on the blackboard,' whispered Miss Gomaz.

'It's . . . it's going to the lavatory,' gasped Mrs Hicks. 'In a bin. I can't believe my eyes.'

They were just pressing their noses to the window-pane to get a closer look when Ms Wiz glanced up. Those at the front of the class could hear a slight hum coming from her direction.

'Miss Gomaz! Miss Gomaz!' said Mrs Hicks. 'My nose! It's stuck to the glass!'

'Mine too!' cried Miss Gomaz, trying to pull back from the window-pane. 'Ouch! That hurts!'

It was at that moment that the bell rang for afternoon break. Soon the teachers were surrounded by laughing children.

'Don't just stand there, you horrible children,' screamed Mrs Hicks. 'Get help quickly.'

'No need,' said Ms Wiz, who had joined the children in the playground. She tapped the glass. Miss Gomaz and Mrs Hicks fell back, free at last.

'It must have been the frost,' said Ms Wiz, with an odd little smile.

'Frost?' said Miss Gomaz, rubbing her nose. 'At this time of year? Don't talk daft.'

'It's only September,' said Mrs Hicks.

'Yes,' said Ms Wiz. 'What funny old weather we've been having, don't you think?'

Chapter Four

Herbert Takes a Wrong Turning

It was during an art lesson that Class
Three were first given an idea where Ms
Wiz came from.

She had asked the children to draw an
imaginary building. The project was
called 'The House of My Dreams'.

Jack drew a house that looked like
Wembley Stadium. It had a football
ground in the living-room and all the
walls were slanted like skateboard ramps.

Caroline drew the mansion that she
would have when she became a film star.
It had a huge lawn and swimming-pool.

In every room, there was a cocktail cabinet for drinks.

Podge drew Buckingham Palace made out of milk chocolate and fudge.

Katrina drew a strange, dark cottage in a wood. Cats with shining eyes stood guard on each side of the front door and bats flew in and out of its old thatched roof. She called it 'Ms Wiz's Magic Cottage'.

When Katrina finished the picture, Ms Wiz laughed. 'It's lovely,' she said, 'but not at all like where I really live.'

'Where *do* you live?' asked Katrina. The entire class grew quiet. Somehow no one had ever dared ask Ms Wiz about herself before.

'I live in a flat a long, long way away,' said Ms Wiz. 'At a place where almost certainly none of you have been. It's on the outskirts of town.'

'Can we come and visit you during the holidays?' asked Jack.

'During the holidays,' said Ms Wiz, 'I'm doing other things. That's my job – to go wherever a little magic is needed. Wherever –' she smiled '– things need shaking up a little.'

'You've certainly shaken things up at St Barnabas,' said Katrina. 'Does that mean you'll be leaving us soon?'

Ms Wiz smiled. 'Katrina, I'll only leave you when you no longer need me.'

For a moment, there was silence in Class Three. Then Podge put up his hand.

'If you live so far away,' he asked, 'how do you get to school every day? Do you fly on your vacuum cleaner?'

'No,' said Ms Wiz. 'I come by bus.'

If Ms Wiz was a little more serious than usual that afternoon, it was because she was thinking of the evening ahead of her. It was Parents' Evening.

Ms Wiz liked being with children. She didn't even mind being with teachers. But the idea of a whole evening spent in the company of parents made her feel tired already.

'I must remember to keep my spells under control,' she said to herself as she waited for the first parent to arrive. 'Adults aren't like children. Magic seems to upset them.'

The door opened.

'I'm Harris,' said a large man in a suit, who was the first parent to arrive. He shook Ms Wiz firmly by the hand. 'Peter's dad. This – ' he nodded curtly towards a nervous-looking woman standing a pace behind him ' – is Mother.'

Peter? Ms Wiz's mind raced. Who was Peter? Of course – that was Podge's real name.

'Pod – I mean Peter is doing well this term,' she said, glancing at her notes.

'We're not happy,' said Mr Harris

firmly. 'Isn't that right, Mother?'

'It is,' said Mrs Harris. 'We're not happy at all.'

'The lad's gone strange on us,' continued Mr Harris. 'Always got his head in a book. Or talking about school. Asking us questions about this and that when his mother and I are trying to watch telly.'

'Questions all the time,' said Mrs Harris.

'Yak yak yak,' said Mr Harris. 'I'm a busy man. I work at the Town Hall. I want to relax of an evening, not answer questions from my own flesh and blood. That's your job.'

Ms Wiz smiled. 'Perhaps it's a good sign that he's interested in – '

'He's never been interested before. Tea, telly, bed was our way. Nothing wrong with that.' Mr Harris leant forward angrily. 'I've said to Mother and I'll say it to you. I smell a rat – ' (For a horrible moment, Ms Wiz thought he had discovered Herbert, who was asleep up her sleeve) – 'and when Cuthbert Harris smells a rat, heads will roll. Come on, Mother, I'm off.'

Mr Harris stood up and, without another word, walked towards the door. Was it an accident that a banana skin had been left on the floor – or was it a touch of

Ms Wiz magic after all?

'Wooooaaaahhh!'

With a sickening crash, Mr Harris landed on the floor in a heap.

'Oh, Cuthbert!' said Mrs Harris. 'Your best suit!'

Podge's father stood up, red-faced.

'Right! That's it!' he said as he dusted himself down. 'Town Hall's going to hear of this. Heads will roll!'

Ms Wiz sighed as the door slammed behind Mr and Mrs Harris. Yes, she definitely preferred children to parents.

Ms Wiz was not often angry but when, a few days after Parents' Evening, Mr Gilbert brought a School Inspector from the Town Hall into the classroom, there was an unusual sharpness in her tone when she addressed the class.

'Now sit up, Class Three,' she said after the headmaster had left the School Inspector sitting at a little desk at the back of the class. 'Remember we're being inspected by the Town Hall.'

The School Inspector pursed his lips and made a note on the pad in front of him.

It was a quiet lesson without, of course, a hint of magic. Even Hecate the Cat remained hidden in Ms Wiz's bag.

Unfortunately nobody had told Herbert that Class Three was being inspected and Herbert, as luck would have it, decided on this particular moment to explore the classroom.

After a few minutes of the lesson, he

had discovered a new tunnel. It was warm and dark, like a very inviting, old-fashioned chimney.

Who could blame him for wanting to explore it? Rats like chimneys. How was he to know that he was climbing up the left leg of the School Inspector's trousers?

At first the School Inspector twitched. Then he shifted nervously in his seat. Then, as Herbert edged his way past his knee and upwards, the School Inspector stood up.

'Oh . . . oooh . . . .,' he said, patting his thigh. 'What the . . . oh . . . ah . . . ' He hopped around the classroom.

It was then that Herbert decided the chimney was moving around rather too much for comfort – and made for the safety of the School Inspector's underpants.

'AAAARRRRRGGGGGHHHHH!'
The School Inspector tore at his belt, jumped out of his trousers and ran from

the classroom.

Class Three watched in amazement as the half-naked figure sprinted across the playground, out of the school gates and down the road.

Relieved that the earthquake had passed, Herbert emerged nervously from the School Inspector's trousers on the classroom floor.

'Oh, Herbert,' said Ms Wiz. 'You've done it now.'

Chapter Five

An Absolute Disgrace

Mr Gilbert was in a muddle. You might think that Mr Gilbert was always in a muddle, but this was the biggest muddle he had ever been in since he became headmaster of St Barnabas.

He was in such a muddle that his bald head had developed ugly red blotches. His attention would wander during lessons. He had even stopped picking his nose during Assembly.

'I'm on the horns of a dilemma,' he told Mrs Gilbert one evening. 'People keep telling me that Ms Wiz is a disaster. Miss

Gomaz and Mrs Hicks say she's a troublemaker. The School Inspector says her classroom is a health hazard. Mr Harris says heads will roll. They all want me to suspend her before the end-of-term Prizegiving next week.'

'Suspend her then, Henry,' said Mrs Gilbert. 'What's the problem?'

'The problem is that the children of Class Three have won all the prizes this term. It's incredible. That sleepy Caroline has won the Art Prize. Jack has won the Maths Prize. The A for Attitude Award for Good Behaviour has gone to Katrina of all people. Even the appalling Podge has won a Commendation for his story,

"The Enchanted Fudge Cake with a Thick Creamy Milk Chocolate Filling". How on earth can I say, "Well done everyone in Class Three and by the way I'm suspending your teacher"?'

'You'd better do what you think is best,' said Mrs Gilbert. 'But don't allow yourself to be bullied this time.'

'Of course not,' said Mr Gilbert. 'You know where I stand on bullying.'

'Let me guess,' said Mrs Gilbert. 'On the horns of a dilemma?'

'Precisely,' said Mr Gilbert.

'Is it true that you're going to be suspended?' asked Katrina the next day in class. 'Ever since the School Inspector lost his trousers, Mr Gilbert's been giving you some very funny looks.'

'So have Miss Gomaz and Mrs Hicks,' said Jack. 'They look positively happy.'

'My dad's smiling a lot,' said Podge.

'And that's never a good sign.'

'Never you mind about me,' said Ms Wiz. 'I can look after myself.'

'Yeah,' said Simon. 'You can magic 'em. That would show 'em.'

'What have I always said? No unpleasant spells,' said Ms Wiz.

'Oh, Ms,' said Podge. 'Couldn't you just use a bit of magic – just one little spell on Mr Gilbert?'

'Maybe you could change him into a human being,' suggested Jack.

There were cheers around the classroom. Ms Wiz held up her hands. Class Three were quiet.

'No,' she said. 'I refuse to listen to rumours. If the headmaster no longer requires my services, there's nothing to be done about it.'

'Oh yes, there is,' said Jack.

Which is how Class Three's Great Plan came into being.

End-of-term Prizegiving was the most important event of the term for St Barnabas. It took place on the last day before the holidays and everybody was there.

On the platform in the School Hall sat Mr Gilbert, the School Inspector, all the teachers and the Lady Mayoress, a large, impressive woman who was wearing a large, impressive hat. In the audience were the children with their parents.

Mr Gilbert had just finished his end-of-term speech which, give or take a couple of pathetic jokes, was the same as every end-of-term speech he had made for the last ten years.

'Now,' he said, 'I would like to ask the Lady Mayoress – ' Mr Gilbert gave a simpering little bow in her direction ' – to present the prizes. First, the Art Prize to Caroline Smith of Class Three.'

There was polite applause as Caroline collected her prize.

'The Maths Prize has been won by Jack Beddows of Class Three.'

Jack collected his prize, giving a modest wave to his supporters from the platform.

'The A for Attitude Award for Good Behaviour,' Mr Gilbert tried to keep the disbelief out of his voice, 'to Katrina O'Brien of Class Three.' Katrina actually gave a little curtsey to the Lady Mayoress as she was presented with her award.

'And Specially Commended for his essay, "The Enchanted Fudge Cake with a Thick Creamy Milk Chocolate Filling" – Peter Harris of Class Three.'

Podge climbed the steps to the platform. But instead of collecting his prize from the Lady Mayoress, he took the microphone from the astonished headmaster.

'Everyone in Class Three wants to thank Ms Wiz,' he announced. 'She's the best teacher we've ever had – '

'Give me that microphone, boy,' said Mr Gilbert, chasing Podge around the stage.

'WE HOPE SHE NEVER EVER LEAVES!' shouted Podge. 'Don't we, Class Three?'

At that moment, the children of Class Three stood up and started cheering. Several of them produced banners, reading 'MS WIZ IS MAGIC' and 'NO SACK FOR MS WIZ', which had been smuggled into the hall.

'You can stop that right now, Peter,' said Podge's father, Mr Harris, advancing towards the platform. 'I'm going to give you a proper larrupping when you get home.'

There was a humming sound from the back of the stage where Ms Wiz was sitting quietly.

Suddenly Mr Harris had turned into a strange pig-like animal.

'Goodness,' said Miss Gomaz. 'He's turned into a warthog.'

'Surely not,' said Mrs Hicks. 'Warthogs don't have those funny little tusks. He looks more like a wild boar to me.'

'Never mind that,' shouted Mr Gilbert. 'We have a full-scale riot on our baaa – ' in a flash, there was a sheep standing in the headmaster's place.

By now the entire school was chanting, 'We want Ms Wiz! We want Ms Wiz!'

Ms Wiz stood up and Podge gave her the microphone.

'I think,' she said firmly, 'that we should continue Prizegiving in half an hour. I'd like to see Class Three in their classroom now, please.'

She made her way through the audience, which was now silent.

'Phone the police, Miss Gomaz,' hissed Mrs Hicks.

Ms Wiz glanced over her shoulder.

Suddenly where Miss Gomaz and Mrs Hicks had been standing, there were two grey geese, making a furious gobbling noise.

'That was very kind of you, Class Three,' said Ms Wiz, when all the children had gathered in the classroom. 'But the fact is, I'm leaving St Barnabas anyway.'

There was silence in the classroom.

'Why?' asked Katrina eventually.

'After all that,' muttered Podge.

'I go where magic is needed,' said Ms Wiz. 'Where things need livening up.

Today you've proved that you no longer need me. You're the best class in the school.'

'We won't be, without you,' said Caroline.

'Yes, you will,' said Ms Wiz. 'Wait and see.'

'We'll miss you,' said Jack, serious for once.

'No, you won't because – '

The class looked expectantly at Ms Wiz. Caroline managed to stop sniffling at the back of the class.

' – because I'll be back,' said Ms Wiz.

'When?'

'Where?'

'Next term?'

Ms Wiz held up her hands.

'I'll come back and see each one of you,' she said with a smile. 'When you least expect it, when you need a spot of Ms Wiz magic in your life, I'll be there.'

'Every one of us?' asked Simon.

'Every one of you,' said Ms Wiz. 'And I'll bring Hecate the Cat *and* Herbert.'

Ms Wiz gathered up her bag. She swung her leg over her vacuum-cleaner, like a cowboy about to ride out of town on his horse.

'Go back to the School Hall and finish Prizegiving,' she said. 'You'll find everything's back to normal.'

Ms Wiz hovered in mid-air by the classroom window.

'See you soon, Class Three,' she said and flew off across the playground and over the School Hall.

'Oh no,' said Jack as the class filed back into the hall. 'Look who Ms Wiz has forgotten.'

On the platform beside Mr Gilbert, the School Inspector and the Lady Mayoress, who were looking as if nothing strange had happened at all, stood two grey geese.

51

'She'll *have* to come back now,' said Katrina.

'No unpleasant spells,' said Podge.

They heard a familiar hum from outside the hall.

'Gobble gobble gobble – absolute disgrace,' said Miss Gomaz.

Jack sighed.

'I think I preferred them as geese,' he said.

Terence Blacker
In Stitches with Ms Wiz £2.99

The day Ms Wiz becomes a doctor, the hospital is in for a surprise!

Her stethoscope plays disco music . . . A pickled appendix escapes from its jar . . . And the children's ward is overrun by mice . . . The medical staff are suspicious, the consultant is confused. Everyone else?

They're in STITCHES!

Ms Wiz is back!

Terence Blacker
In Control Ms Wiz? £2.99

Ms Wiz has got a new job. She works in a library, where she can *really* bring books to life . . .

. . . a talent she needs when the council tries to close it down.

Pretty soon rabbits, a champion hamburger eater and a right royal couple start rampaging around . . .

Can they save the library?

Can Ms Wiz keep them in control?

Terence Blacker
You're Nicked, Ms Wiz £2.99

First Lizzie Thompson's cat. Then Lizzie herself. Who will be next to go missing?

PC Boote hopes it will be Ms Wiz.

As for Ms Wiz . . . she's got other plans.

Like trying to find the missing pair. And finding out who's behind the whole mystery . . .

Eva Ibbotson
**The Worm and the Toffee-Nosed Princess
and other stories of monsters** £2.50

Why did the giant, hairy worm eat the snooty princess? What happened to
the silly dog who dared to annoy a Frid? And how did the three Scotsmen deal
with a sheep-eating Boobrie?

Find out the answers to these, and other questions in this collection of funny
tales about monsters, written specially for readers who are progressing from
picture books to longer stories.

James Riordan
**The Boy Who Turned Into a Goat
and other stories of magical changes** £2.50

Catherine warned her brother not to drink the water in the forest. 'For if you do,' she said, 'you will turn into a goat.'

Boys like Sean rarely take notice of the things their sisters say – but, oh, how he wished he had!

Read about the fishermen who became crows, the princess who turned into an apple, the magical vinegar jar and other amazing tales of transformations from around the world!

Ideal for readers who are progressing from picture books to longer stories – and for reading aloud.

Alison Uttley
Foxglove Tales £3.50
Illustrated by Shirley Felts

'Her gentle evocation of rural life has lost none of its charm for the present generation of young readers and listeners. An ideal book for storytelling.'
RECENT CHILDREN'S FICTION

Rainbow Tales £3.50
Illustrated by Shirley Hughes

A wonderful collection of eleven tales which capture the magic and beauty of the countryside. Meet such delightful characters as Sam Pig, John Barleycorn, the clever Mr. Fox and many more.

Mick Gowar
Brenda-The-Do-It-Yourself-Brownie £2.99

Brenda is sure that being a Brownie is the most exciting thing in the whole world. But the day after her seventh birthday she's told that the Brownies are full until September.

Brenda can't wait that long. So she decides to start her own pack with little brother Sean, Sylvia from next door and Tigger the cat. They'll do all the things real Brownies do . . .

It's not Brenda's fault if they all go wrong!

All Pan books are available at your local bookshop or newsagent, or can be ordered direct from the publisher. Indicate the number of copies required and fill in the form below.

Send to: **CS Department, Pan Books Ltd., P.O. Box 40, Basingstoke, Hants.   RG21 2YT.**

or phone: 0256 469551 (Ansaphone), quoting title, author and Credit Card number.

Please enclose a remittance* to the value of the cover price plus: 60p for the first book plus 30p per copy for each additional book ordered to a maximum charge of £2.40 to cover postage and packing.

*Payment may be made in sterling by UK personal cheque, postal order, sterling draft or international money order, made payable to Pan Books Ltd.

Alternatively by Barclaycard/Access:

Card No.

Signature:

Applicable only in the UK and Republic of Ireland.

While every effort is made to keep prices low, it is sometimes necessary to increase prices at short notice. Pan Books reserve the right to show on covers and charge new retail prices which may differ from those advertised in the text or elsewhere.

NAME AND ADDRESS IN BLOCK LETTERS PLEASE:

....

Name———————————————————————————

Address—————————————————————————————

————————————————————————————————

————————————————————————————————

————————————————————————————————

3/87